MW00948319

The Sock Animals:

Tiger's New Friends

The Sock Animal Series:

Tiger's New Friends

Tiger's Vacation

For ordering information, see back page.

The Sock Animals:

Tiger's New Friends

Photography and story

by

Ann Jacobs Mooney

THE SOCK ANIMALS: TIGER'S NEW FRIENDS. Copyright ©
1992 by Ann Jacobs Mooney. All rights reserved. Reproduction of
photography or text in any manner prohibited without written
permission by author. For information regarding permission, write
to Jamondas Press, P.O. Box 3325, Ann Arbor, Michigan 48106.

Library of Congress Catalog Card Number 91- 76359.
ISBN 0-9631035-0-4

Design and typesetting by Lisa Climer-Harding.

First Edition   2 3 4 5 6 7 8 9 10
Printed in the United States of America

This book is dedicated
to Danny
and his wonderful imagination.

Once upon a time, there were two very good friends. These friends were made from socks. One was a monkey and one was an elephant, and they lived with a little boy who loved them very much.

Monkey and Ellie the Elephant always played together. They swung from an old apple tree in the little boy's backyard.

They played hide and seek around
the flowers on the kitchen table.

One day the little boy asked his mother to sew him a new sock animal. He wanted a tiger.

So she made him a tiger with a friendly face and beautiful black stripes. As soon as the little boy saw Tiger, he loved his new animal just as much as he loved his old ones.

Tiger wanted very much to be friends with Monkey and Ellie. He watched them playing happily together. Tiger hoped Monkey and Ellie would ask him to play, too.

So he watched and watched, and he hoped and hoped. But Monkey and Ellie never asked Tiger to play with them.

The little boy had a favorite rock in his mother's garden that he called his Thinking Rock. It was perfect for sitting on and thinking important thoughts.

One day, Monkey and Ellie were playing on the Thinking Rock.

Monkey said to Ellie, "Do you want to ask Tiger to play with us today?"

"No," said Ellie. "He's different than we are."

Monkey was confused. "You and I are different, and we're friends."

Ellie thought for a minute. "Well, Tiger doesn't have purple eyes like mine."

"Silly elephant," Monkey laughed, "my eyes are red, and you play with me!"

Ellie laughed too. "Maybe I'm just not ready for a new friend yet. Or maybe we need a new Thinking Rock to figure this out."

Meanwhile, Tiger was lonely and sad. He climbed the little boy's apple tree all by himself.

He wanted a ride on the little boy's swing, but Tiger had no one to push him. He kept wishing Monkey and Ellie would be his friends.

One day, Monkey's little cousin Cassie came to visit. Cassie loved to climb.

She saw a tall yellow sunflower in
the garden behind the boy's house. She
wanted to smell that big pretty flower.
So Cassie climbed and climbed.

Suddenly Monkey heard Cassie
calling to him. "Cousin Monkey! I can't
get down! I'm up too high!"
Monkey, Ellie, and Tiger looked up.
They saw little Cassie hanging onto the
top of the huge sunflower.

Monkey and Ellie didn't know
what to do. Cassie was very scared.
Then they all saw Tiger slowly climbing
up the tall sunflower. Tiger was going to
try to rescue little Cassie!

Cassie was very happy to see Tiger. He carried her all the way down the sunflower. She kept hanging on very tightly to Tiger's ear.

Tiger brought Cassie over to Monkey. Monkey hugged his little cousin.

"Thank you, Tiger," said Monkey. "You were very good to help Cassie. But Ellie and I have not been very friendly to you. Why did you help *my* cousin, even when I have not been nice to *you*?"

Tiger smiled. "Because Cassie was scared, and I wanted to make her happy again."

Monkey said to Ellie, "Tiger is a very special friend." And Ellie agreed.

From that day on, Monkey, Ellie, and Tiger were all the best of friends. They laughed and played together in the garden full of marigolds.

They loved to swing together on
the little boy's tire in the old apple tree.

They were all very happy, especially Tiger, who finally had his sock friends.

And whenever Monkey's cousin Cassie came to visit, she loved to play with her favorite friend, the kind and wonderful Tiger.

The End

Acknowledgment

First published through the support of
KELLY ALYN JACKSON,
Allen Park, Michigan,
a seven-year-old and future author.

Directions for Making

- Tiger

- Monkey

- Ellie the Elephant

Directions for Making

TIGER

Materials
• One pair of red-heeled socks • Stuffing (polyester fiberfill, nylon stockings, etc.)
• Trim: black embroidery thread, buttons or felt (optional), cardboard (optional)

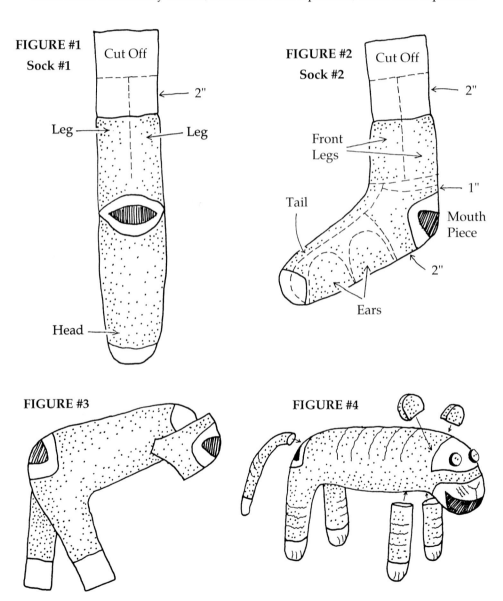

FIGURE #1

Sock #1

Cut Off

← 2"

Leg →

← Leg

Head →

FIGURE #2

Sock #2

Cut Off

← 2"

Front Legs →

← 1"

Mouth Piece

Tail

2"

Ears

FIGURE #3

FIGURE #4

Please read ALL of the instructions before beginning to make Tiger.

BODY AND BACK LEGS: Cut sock #1, leaving 2″ of white cuff (the foot) attached to the brown. Stuff only the head and body sections of sock #1. Turn back legs inside out and seam each leg, leaving crotch area and feet areas open. Turn legs right side out; stuff. Do not do final stitching (at top and feet) until you cut front legs, in case adjustments need to be made to get all legs the same length.

FRONT LEGS: Cut front legs out of sock #2. Turn legs inside out and seam, leaving tops and bottoms open. Turn legs right side out; stuff. Make sure all legs are even. If legs are too long or uneven, Tiger won't stand up. (If you want to shorten back legs, remove the white cuff "foot" section. Then shorten brown part of the leg and reattach the white foot.) Complete all length adjustments. Attach front legs. For stiffer, rounder feet, insert 1¹/₂″ circles of heavy cardboard in bottoms before seaming. Add more stuffing as needed at top of back legs and crotch before closing.

FACE: Cut mouth section from heel area of sock #2, with 1″ of brown on one side of the white heel section, and 2″ of brown on the other side. Fit this piece over the stuffed head section as shown in Figure #3. Sew just the top edge of this mouth piece smoothly over the middle line of the white toe of the stuffed "body sock" underneath. Stuff this muzzle section to desired fullness. There will be loose extra brown material on sides and underneath. Take tucks along sides and under chin as necessary. Folding all cut edges of this mouth piece under, sew the rest of the mouth piece onto the body sock.

EARS: Cut ears from the second sock as shown. Turn them inside out and sew a seam about ¹/₂″ from the edge, leaving the bottom open. Turn right side out, stuff, and attach.

TAIL: Cut a 1¹/₂″ strip (double thickness) from sock #2, with the end in the white section for a white tip. Turn inside out and seam, leaving bottom open. Turn right side out, stuff and attach.

TRIM: For eyes, use buttons or felt. For young children, embroider eyes, as buttons can be pulled off and become a choking hazard. Embroider black stripes on back, tail, legs, and above eyes. Thick black stitches on the front of white feet make great claws. A black "Y" coming up from his red mouth will look like a tiger nose. Add black whiskers for the finishing touch!

© Jamondas Press, 1992

Directions for Making

MONKEY

Materials
• One pair of red-heeled socks • Stuffing (polyester fiberfill, nylon stockings, etc.)
• Trim: black embroidery thread, buttons or felt (optional) • Red yarn (optional)

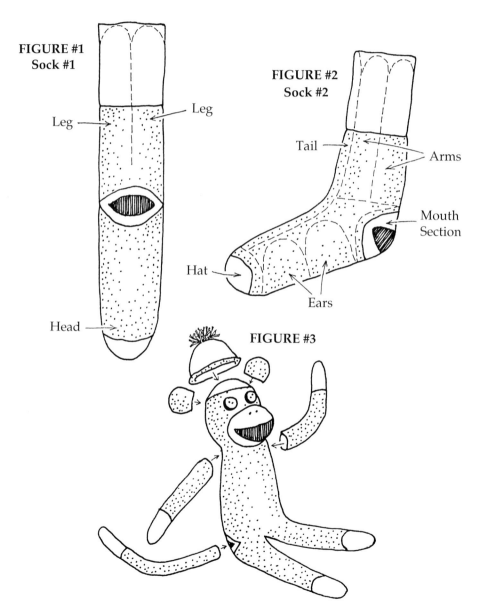

FIGURE #1
Sock #1

Leg

Leg

Head

FIGURE #2
Sock #2

Tail

Arms

Mouth Section

Hat

Ears

FIGURE #3

Please read ALL of the instructions before beginning to make Monkey.

BODY AND LEGS: Cut sock #1, making center cut stop about $1^{1}/2''$ before you get to the white heel section. Stuff the head and body sections. Turn legs inside out and seam each leg, leaving crotch area and feet areas open. Turn legs right side out; stuff. Finish seaming the crotch. Decide how long you want the white ribbed foot area. Some people like small white sections for feet, while others leave all of the white ribbed section on. Trim if you wish, and seam the foot areas.

ARMS: Cut the upper part of sock #2 into two arm pieces. Again, decide how much white ribbed section looks good for the "hands" area. Most people make the arms shorter than the legs, so you may want to trim off 1" or 2" of the white section of the arms. Turn inside out and seam, rounding the ends. Turn right side out, stuff, and attach the arms.

FACE: Cut the heel from the second sock, leaving a brown edge around the white. Folding edges under, fasten it on to the lower part of the face, whip-stitching around the bottom. Stuff and finish sewing around top. Running a stitch of either black or white across the middle of the lips completes the mouth. Sew dark stitches for nostrils. A tie of yarn or heavy thread may be used around the neck to make the head area rounder.

EARS: Cut ears from the second sock as shown in Figure #2. Turn them inside out and sew a seam about $^{1}/2''$ from the edge, leaving bottom open. Turn right side out, stuff, and attach.

EYES: Sew on eyes: use buttons, felt, or embroider with black thread. (For young children, embroider eyes, as buttons can be pulled off and become a choking hazard.)

TAIL: Cut a 1" strip (double thickness); taper to end in white cuff section. Turn inside out and seam. Turn right side out, stuff and attach.

CAP: (Optional) Cut off toe of sock #2, leaving $^{1}/2''$ of brown to roll for a brim. Red pompom can be added to top.

TRIM: (Optional) There are many variations of this basic pattern. Remember that for very young children, decorations that could be pulled off should not be used. But for older children, decorations can be either pompoms, yarn or bells. Jackets, vests and skirts are also used for Monkey's clothing.

ELLIE the ELEPHANT

Materials
• One pair of red-heeled socks • Stuffing (polyester fiberfill, nylon stockings, etc.)
• Trim: black embroidery thread, buttons or felt (optional), cardboard (optional)

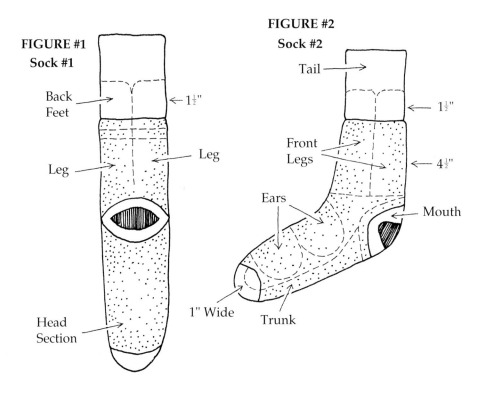

FIGURE #1
Sock #1

Back Feet

Leg

Leg

$1\frac{1}{2}$"

Head Section

1" Wide

FIGURE #2
Sock #2

Tail

Front Legs

Ears

Mouth

Trunk

$1\frac{1}{2}$"

$4\frac{1}{2}$"

FIGURE #3

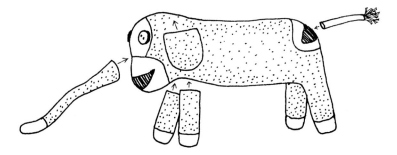

Please read ALL of the instructions before beginning to make Ellie.

HEAD AND BODY: Cut sock #1, making center cut stop $1^1/_2''$ from white of heel. To shape the head, stuff the foot of the sock firmly and tie off loosely at neck with yarn or ribbon. Finish stuffing body.

LEGS: Turn back legs inside out; seam, leaving crotch and bottoms of legs open. Turn right side out and stuff. Don't add white until front legs are finished to allow for adjustment to get all legs the same length. Cut sock #2. Front legs should have about $4^1/_2''$ of brown and $1^1/_2''$ of white. Turn inside out; seam. Turn right side out and stuff, leaving tops and bottoms open. Insert $1^1/_2''$ circles of stiff cardboard in bottoms of feet; sew feet closed. Attach front legs. Adjust back legs' length to match front legs. Put stiff circles in white back foot sections, stuff, and add to brown legs. Add more stuffing to crotch section if necessary. Sew crotch and bottoms of feet closed.

MOUTH: Cut out the heel section from sock #2, leaving $^1/_2''$ of brown attached to the white. Stuff lightly and sew onto bottom of head.

TRUNK: Cut trunk so that it is 1" wide (double thickness), widening to 2" at brown end. Round the wide end. Fold inside out. Seam along one edge and around narrow end, leaving wide end open. Turn right side out and stuff. Sew onto head on the front of the face (which may also be over some of the white of the mouth section) with the seam underneath.

EARS: Cut two pieces in shape of ears. Seam and turn right side out. Sew on sides of Ellie's head.

EYES: Sew on moving eyes, buttons, felt or embroider with black thread. (For young children, embroider or sew on felt eyes for safety.)

TAIL: Cut a small 3" x 1" piece of white ribbed sock material. Roll it up lengthwise and seam it smoothly. Attach one end to Ellie, and with thread, tie the other end off about $^1/_2''$ from the end.

TRIM: Trim is optional. A fringed strip of bright material can be placed over the back, or tassels may be sewn on. Always remember that decorations such as bells, beads or buttons should not be used on toys for very young children. They can be pulled off and present choking hazards. However, for older children, rickrack, little bells, ribbons or beads give the toy a more festive, circus-like appearance.

Ordering Information

Look for *The Sock Animals Series* books and gift packs in quality bookstores, craft stores, and catalogs. They also may be ordered direct. Prices are as follows:

Tiger's New Friends

$7.95 plus $1.95 shipping and handling. This storybook now includes a section with directions for making Tiger, Monkey, and Ellie the Elephant.

Tiger's New Friends Gift Pack

$11.95 plus $2.80 shipping and handling. This specially wrapped package includes the storybook with directions and one pair of red-heeled socks to make one animal.

Tiger's Vacation

$7.95 plus $1.95 shipping and handling. This storybook also includes a section with directions for making Tiger and two new sock animals: Jake the Rattlesnake and Hobby the Horse.

Tiger's Vacation Gift Pack

$11.95 plus $2.80 shipping and handling. This package includes the storybook with directions and one pair of red-heeled socks to make one animal.

Send checks or money orders to:

Jamondas Press
Post Office Box 3325
Ann Arbor, Michigan 48106

If using MasterCard or Visa, you may call our toll-free order line: 1-800-223-7873. Michigan residents must include current sales tax.